The Family That
Time Forgot

*With compliments
of the Prince Regent's son.*

The Family That Time Forgot

John Haywood

VANTAGE PRESS
New York

Published by Vantage Press, Inc.
516 West 34th Street, New York, New York 10001

Manufactured in the United States of America
ISBN: 0-533-13871-X

Library of Congress Catalog Card No.: 01-126075

0 9 8 7 6 5 4 3 2 1

The world forgetting, by the world forgot.

Alexander Pope
Eloisa to Abelard

Contents

Preface

Today, on the outskirts of Petersburg, Virginia, there stands an old Anglican church, now commonly known as Old Blandford Church. It was erected in 1735, but it was abandoned around 1800. In the year 1841, the following lines by an anonymous author were found written on its walls.

Thou art crumbling to the dust,
old pile,
Thou art hastening to thy fall,
And 'round thee in thy loneliness
Clings the ivy to thy wall.
The worshipers are scattered
now,
Who knelt before thy shrine,
And silence reigns where anthems
rose
In days of "Auld Lang Syne."

And sadly sighs the wandering
wind
Where oft in years gone by
Prayers rose from many hearts
to Him
The Highest of the High;
The tramp of many a busy foot
That sought thy aisles is o'er
And many a weary heart around
Is still forevermore.

How doth ambition's hope take
wing.
How droops the spirit now;
We hear the distant city's din.
The dead are mute below.
The sun that shone upon their
paths
Now gilds their lonely graves;
The zephyrs which once fanned
their brows
The grass above them waves.

Oh! Could we call the many back
Who've gathered here in vain—
Who've careless roved where we
do now,
Who'll never meet again;
How would our very hearts be
stirred
To meet the earnest gaze
Of the lovely and the beautiful
The lights of other days.

Some have attributed these lines to the Irish playwright
Tyrone Power, others to Edgar Allan Poe, yet there exists no
evidence, whatsoever, to substantiate these opinions.

The account that follows attempts to explain this
enigma. It also attempts to bring due attention to the exis-
tence of a family, known at that time by the name of Russell,
whose acts once altered the course of Western civilization,
irrevocably, and as a consequence, disappeared from the
pages of recorded history.

This infamous dynasty possessed an estate, identified
herein only as Russell House, that unmentionable manor
that once existed in the vicinity. Rumor contends that it

burned to the ground after being struck by lightning, divinely inspired. Others say it once existed on the site of battlefields outside the city and was destroyed in the last devastating conflict, which led to the defeat of the Confederacy in 1865.

Some who read this narrative will dismiss it as humbuggery. Others will give it more serious thought. Is it not true that even today, with our scientific knowledge, some extraordinary events still defy explanation? Nevertheless, sites mentioned herein may still be visited to this very day. And some claim to have felt the echoes of Russell House from the past, but that is really irrelevant. The author asks but that you read this with candor, and then decide for yourself your own opinion.

The Family That Time Forgot

1
A Stranger's Warning

It was a typical October day. The forest was aflame in all the bright colors of autumn. Even though the sun was shining brightly, periodic breezes reminded one that it wouldn't be long before the onset of winter.

Mile after mile I had continued, ever since leaving Richmond that morning. It really wasn't far to go, considering the great distance I had thence traveled, all the way from Boston. I had doubts that I was going in the right direction, ever since leaving the main road, which goes from Richmond southward for some twenty miles to Petersburg.

At length, a man driving a wagon approached. "Good morning to you, sir," I began.

"Good morning," he responded, "Lost your way?" he continued, drawing amusement it seemed, as only natives can, at a stranger misguided.

"Not exactly. Is this the way to Russell House?"

"Russell House?" A suspicious frown crossed his face. "Do you know them?"

"Yes," I responded, somewhat irritated at the interrogation.

"It is farther on, about a mile and a half, but take my advice, sir, and keep on riding, for no good will come to you at Russell House." With that, he abruptly drove on.

Rude fellow, I thought, as I continued onward. *Russell House.* The name reverberated in my mind.

This was the occasion of my first visit to Russell House. Indeed this was my first journey out of Massachusetts. I was going to visit my kinsmen, the Russells, distant cousins, whom I had never met. They were descendants of my great-great-grandfather, who had arrived in America many years ago in Virginia. I suppose it really was an exaggeration to call them kinsmen, cousins, for the relationship was so far removed as to not exist at all.

Yet, because of our common ancestry, we continued the practice of periodic correspondence. Aside from casual knowledge and the customary greetings at Christmas, we knew very little of this family. It was always this group in Virginia that had an aura of intrigue surrounding them. Even though our family had originally arrived in Virginia, the part that migrated to Massachusetts prospered and grew, whereas, those who remained in Virginia had been less fortunate. When I say less fortunate, I speak not of wealth and financial success, of which knowledge thereof, I had none at all. We had a vague knowledge that several misfortunes had beset them, among them, I believe, a smallpox decimation in the last century. Also, I believe a number of them had perished in the Revolution. Nevertheless, should this be true or not, it was a fact that those at Russell House comprised the last of this family in Virginia.

These thoughts occupied my mind as I continued onward. I soon left the dense forest and came upon a clearing when, to my surprise, a woman on a white steed crossed the road farther ahead, going at great speed, as if chasing someone or something. She paid no attention to my presence, or else she didn't notice me because she never once turned her head in my direction. A beautiful woman she was, dressed in black. Both horse and rider seemed to be one, as they continued gracefully, her cloak and long, light-brown hair flowing in the air behind her.

I knew by now that I was at last on the estate of Russell House, and continuing a little farther, I came to the large edifice. It was a rather large structure to be so isolated from the nearby civilization. It appeared to be almost three stories high, and the entire house, as far as I could tell, was covered with ivy, except for the windows, of course, which were left exposed.

There were no signs of activity, i.e., horses tied up in the front, but I fancied, as I drew nearer to the house, in one of the uppermost windows, I saw someone, the outline of a man, peering out the window. As I started to gaze upward at the physiognomy, the shade was quickly drawn.

I tied my horse, rapped three times on the door, and was soon admitted by a manservant.

"Good morning," I began. "I'm Richard Randolph from Boston. My cousins, the Russells, are expecting me." I stepped in.

"Yes, sir. I'll tell Master Edward of your arrival. Miss Charlotte isn't in—she's out riding. I'll be back presently." With that, he quit the room.

The servant was soon back, leading a man of my own age to my presence, I noticed he was slightly lame.

"How do you do?" he started, rather coldly, extending his hand. "I'm your cousin Edward. Welcome to Russell House. At long last, we have finally met."

"Yes," I responded. "Isn't it unusual that after so many years of distance between our two families, we have at last bridged the generations?"

He concurred, and we thereupon initiated a conversation consisting of the usual social pleasantries and other topics of no great substance.

Edward was tall, and although of medium frame, he

was well muscled, I guess from the extra activities that country dwellers naturally have. He had light brown hair of medium length, but it was the eyes that caught one's attention immediately. Dark, brown eyes they were, eyes so pensive, they seemed to pierce through one's countenance to the utter depths of one's soul.

Edward finally took his leave, and he indicated to me that I would meet his sister at dinner, which would be at three o'clock. It was my understanding that a long-held custom of Virginia gentry was to take dinner in mid-afternoon, and thence, have a smaller meal at night.

I was then taken to my room. In the intervening period, I had an opportunity to survey the house. It became most evident that much of the home had not been in active use for many years. It was also clear that it was beyond the capacity of any one person to keep the place in a fashion so as to receive guests, because they had only one domestic, from all evidence. In fact I should doubt that any decorative endeavor or the addition of furniture had taken place in thirty years. Therefore, some rooms were closed off, leaving only the ones necessary for the present inhabitants.

At the appointed hour, dinner was served and I beheld Charlotte closely for the first time. She was strikingly beautiful. She had long brown hair and brown eyes that were set in a countenance that portrayed to me the innocence of maidenhood and adolescence in the person of a woman.

After the usual trite pleasantries between us, the conversation that ensued during the meal was very unusual. "I want to convey my condolences to both of you on the loss of your father." (It already was our family's knowledge of his decease some weeks prior to my arrival.) "I know you will find his absence great. By the way, what was his illness?"

"Cousin Richard," Charlotte interjected, ignoring my

4

question, "do you believe that people can be controlled by past events?"

"Definitely," I responded. "All of us are influenced and controlled by historical events. The Revolution is a good example."

"No," she continued, "I speak not of history, but of certain events in the lives of individuals that affect their posterity indefinitely."

"I guess it is conceivable that that could be true. After all, we all are irrevocably predisposed by the decisions and acts of our parents."

"I think I should bring to your attention," Edward said, "that we are rather not liked by the local populace. It has been that way for many years."

"Oh, really?" I responded.

"Yes," he continued. "It dates back to my father, who was rather eccentric in his ways, and, of course, local rumor built it all out of proportion, because the people here are very superstitious."

"You wouldn't think," I countered, "that people in 1841 would still cling to such old-fashioned beliefs."

"Nevertheless," Edward continued, "we find it to our advantage to remain aloof from such a people, inasmuch as their feelings and attitudes remained so toward us."

"Well, I agree with your position wholeheartedly. I would probably do the same if I were in your shoes."

It was during this conversation that I happened to observe Charlotte, looking most pensive and downcast in her spirits. It was her saturnine beauty that caught my attention, for I never had occasion to meet a person with a countenance that made such an impression on my mind. It was on this occasion, I believe, when my heart first experienced its rapturous state when confronted with her visage, and it was thenceforward that whenever my thoughts sought visions of felicity, this image of her came into my mind.

In the late afternoon, I decided that I should examine the grounds immediately behind the premises. In the back lay a garden, one in the English style that usually accompanied stately homes in the South during the Colonial period. The arrangement of the garden and the botanical specimens thereof were of such a conventional nature that I fear any further preoccupation with their descriptions should be considered most trite, except for one object.

In the middle of the garden, where one most often expects a fountain, stood a figure of Virtue, clothed in Roman toga and mounted on a pedestal, the stature of the total object being about eight feet, and at the base was thus inscribed this motto:

> May those who have judged
> others receive equal justice.

I felt most intrigued by this monument, and immediately, several questions sprang to my mind, and I resolved that before I left this place, I should have the answers to my curiosity.

Nevertheless, further contact with the Russells on that day was not forthcoming. I neither saw nor encountered either of them for the remainder of that day. Their whereabouts I did not try to ascertain, for I felt their absence to be an abridgement of their responsibility as hosts. As I was later to learn, this was just one peculiarity of their personalities that others found difficult to understand.

I took supper by myself, which was served by a servant. Shortly thereafter, I fell soundly asleep while thumbing through Wakefield's *The Reign of Charles II*. Thus ended my first day at Russell House.

2

A Sudden Apparition

I slept rather soundly that night. After becoming fully awake and dressed, I started to proceed down the hall towards the stairs. I stopped after a few steps, for I thought I beheld a grayish haze or fog hovering over the staircase. Naturally, I began to observe the fog as it made slow movements in a revolution. To my amazement, the fog continued to revolve and it slowly began to assume the form of a man. The apparition appeared to be clothed in medieval apparel.

It hovered there silently, in mid-air, being about six feet in height. All the while, I stood there in amazement, gazing at what was happening. My feeling was one of curiosity rather than consternation, for I was standing at a distance of some twenty feet away. To be sure, I'm sure I would have felt fear had I come upon this form suddenly, without warning. However, the form indicated no movement in my direction. It simply remained in its original location for about five minutes. Then, without any movement or opening of its mouth, these words came forth from the apparition in a dark, resonant tone: "Richard Randolph, touch not the unclean thing and get thee hence from Russell House."

After uttering this sentence, it promptly disappeared. I continued to stand in my original position for several minutes after this incident, questioning my senses, doubting whether the incident even occurred.

After breakfast, I encountered Charlotte. "Cousin Charlotte, have there ever been sightings of ghosts or other supernatural phenomena in this house?"

"Why do you ask?" she countered.

"I think I've just sighted a spirit."

"Oh, come now. Surely you don't believe in such things? It's just your imagination. Come with me. I want to take you somewhere."

With an affectionate grasp, she took hold of my hand and led me to the stables. Having seen her the other day, I had already concluded her to be an excellent horsewoman, which proved to be true. We rode for a long distance in the countryside. At length we came to an abandoned church.

Charlotte started to explain. "This has been a favorite secret place that I've been coming to for years. But since we're cousins, it is only right that I share it with you. It was once a beautiful church, but around 1800, the congregation of Bruton Parish built a new church in the nearby city, so this place was just abandoned. You can see, of course, that it has fallen into ruins."

It was true, the structure was a manifestation of the decay and ruin that befalls edifices that have experienced permanent human abandonment. The brickwork was starting to crumble and weeds had overgrown everything—the graves were never tended now, these people were forgotten. Their lives, their loves, their misfortunes, and their happinesses—these were insignificant now and time had relegated them to the role of anonymity.

"Our family once worshiped here, but when the congregation moved, we never went along into the city. I guess you could say this place has a special attraction for me. Have you ever thought how structures themselves are so much like the people they shelter and accommodate? That with disuse, as with the dis-use of one's limbs, they will wither

8

and perish? I should hate to wither and perish, Richard. In other words, I fear death. It is an abomination to me, something I would like to avoid, if I could."

"But wouldn't we all, if we could?"

"Some can, I am told."

"I've never heard of that. In what way?" I questioned.

"My father always told me that some can survive death, in a spiritual sense, that is, and spend eternity in a blissful state, yet others, because of some misfortune, are doomed for eternity, not in a fiery hell, but rather, to seek solace and succor for their mourning souls. Even the thought of this depresses me."

"Let's not dwell on such morbid thoughts," I quickly answered. "I think you are the most beautiful woman I have ever met, and to know you are my cousin is even more flattering."

I felt her soft hair, angelic hair it seemed to me, and we embraced with a kiss that I wished would last for an eternity. It was clear to me that I would be looking forward to future visits to that place.

While we were at the church, I intended to ask her to show me her family's plot, but because I feared a return to her morbid and melancholy recollections, I refrained.

We returned to Russell House shortly thereafter. I wanted to resume my conversation with Charlotte, but I was unable to find her. She wasn't in her room, and I searched throughout the house, all to no avail. She was also not in the garden; therefore, I reconciled myself to another day of self-entertainment and solitude.

My thoughts were continually on Charlotte, and the more I thought of her and the things she said, the more curiosity and questioning I began to entertain concerning the inhabitants of Russell House. Once again, I felt a reassurance that this would be resolved prior to my departure.

9

3

Edward's Mysterious Illness

Several days passed in the same manner as the preceding ones. As can be noticed, both Charlotte and her brother were by nature very reclusive, only her brother more so. I very rarely had encounters with Edward. He had a very introverted personality, and he never made any attempt to develop any kind of rapport with me.

It was very evident that he was suffering from some kind of illness, the nature of which, I know not. I never really had an experience whereby I could judge his personality and temperament or ascertain the type of illness he was afflicted with, until one day he was visited by his physician from the nearby city. It was my understanding that the two Russells never left the estate, no, not even to go into the nearby city, so naturally, when either required medical attention, it became necessary for the physician to come to them.

On one such visit, Dr. Jeremiah Jackson, a kindly, elderly gentleman, came out to attend to Edward. Upon my introducing myself and engaging in some friendly conversation, he invited me to a social gathering of his. I was thoroughly impressed with his gentle manner. He was escorted to Edward's room. After about an hour, Edward, Charlotte, and Dr. Jackson proceeded to the front for the physician's departure. All the while, Edward was berating the doctor, following him to the door, with Charlotte following meekly behind.

Edward was screaming at the top of his lungs continually at the doctor: "I have no sympathy with quackery nor with pseudo-science, and I will not tolerate charlatans attending me, claiming to be engaged in the practice of medicine. In my opinion, physicians are here to satisfy the needs of their patients. When they cease to satisfy this need, then they are to be dismissed like any other servant."

At the conclusion of this vocal demonstration, he hobbled back to his room. Dr. Jackson, naturally perturbed by this exhibition, left without further ado.

Charlotte attempted to explain all of the foregoing in the following manner: "Don't bother to worry or to think about what happened. It's really insignificant. After you've stayed here for a while, you won't be bothered or disturbed by the strange happenings that occur in this place."

"Tell me," I inquired, "with what illness does Edward suffer?"

"It is an illness that is terminal," she replied. "Physicians know not the cause nor any effective treatment for it. In fact, they do not even have a name for it. All they do know is that it is eventually terminal. Perhaps that should explain to you the reason for Edward's outburst."

"Indeed it does," I said.

"Furthermore," she continued, "if I were you, I wouldn't bother to waste time in responding to that invitation. Stigma is attached to Russell House, and you will be shunned by the people here like the plague."

"Surely the enlightened people of the community are not influenced by such superstition and beliefs of malediction?"

"They're the worst ones. Such people preach Christian charity and supposedly are exemplary examples of their

11

faith, but it is 'slop,' which they can be expected to serve up repeatedly. As far as 'corn' is concerned, here are a few grains thus: avoid them and their hypocrisy and accept any effort of yours to be exactly what it is—casting your pearls before swine. But maybe that is too much corn for one meal." She started sobbing. "Go on and take the slop." Crying, she ran from the room.

It is true that there was some type of estrangement between Russell House and the outside world. This feeling was most apparent in the attitude of people. There were never visitors to Russell House, except the physician, whose visits, of course, were ones of responsibility rather than desire. Even the servants were very distant from the masters of the estate. I speak not of the distance that is naturally inherent in a master-servant relationship, but of an emotional, a mental distance, which was difficult to comprehend. Only very few of the servants living there came in contact with the Russells. Of the others, it seemed they lived their lives completely separate, untouched by Russell House, as if in another world. They could best be described as an invisible presence, always there in case of need, but always detached from personal involvement and contact.

Often, I felt even the flora on the estate differed from that of the outside world. At times, when I had occasion to leave the estate or to go near the boundaries thereof, it seemed to me that the trees and the vegetation belonging to Russell House gave the impression of mourning. Their physical appearances seemed mute yearnings for transplantation to a more favorable plot of earth, for it seemed that in their present abode they possessed the state of being accursed.

I first began to dismiss this thinking as mere imagination such as wonderings of human thoughts will produce when allowed to roam freely at will. But, as I was to learn later, my perception and thinking was stable and sound during these periods, and as I was also to learn, these occurrences were insignificant when compared to the knowledge that was to be revealed to me at a later time.

4

Ghostly Revels

Since most of the time I was left alone and thence to seek my own pleasure and occupation of time, I decided, in my own private way, to pursue and ascertain for myself the true history of Russell House and the inhabitants thereof.

Autumn seems the time of year when the earth can exhibit its own emotions. All the colors of the earth are alive in a jubilant manner, yet it is a jubilance marked by melancholy and negativism. The colors of autumn seem to rejoice in this fashion, knowing that soon the world will be in the death-like state of winter.

This environment of autumn seemed to lift my spirits somewhat on that day. Charlotte and her brother were hibernating in their usual manner; therefore, with no distractions, I decided to peruse the countryside, and first, to go to that old church with its cemetery to see what I could find. After riding a short way, I soon came upon the place, now resembling more a skeleton of an edifice than anything else, with its tenants lying unkempt in close proximity.

As I sat astride my horse observing the scene, I couldn't help but think of the attitudes of people toward their loved ones lost in death. To be sure, after the demise of a close relative, the thought of that one is ever in one's mind. Visits are made regularly to the grave, etc., but a few years pass, and other relatives die, and they in turn pass away, and thoughts of those gone before perish with them. Then, thoughts of them, even their memory, are lost to all posterity forever. Such was the case of those remaining at Russell House.

If only stones could talk, what things I would probably have heard! There, looking at the tombstone of a Sir William Mosely, *What would you tell me, Sir William?* I thought. I laughed, with melancholy. The stone would have to speak, for Sir William had long since returned to dust.

At length, perusing the grounds, I came upon the Russell plot. After dismounting, I glanced over the stones, not believing what I saw—there were *only women* interred there. I made sure to take a closer look, but it was true, only feminine names, none masculine at all. Mary, Elizabeth, Abigail, etc., all Russells—but, *no men*. One epitaph struck my interest:

"Here lies Abigail Russell,
born 23 March 1747
departed this life 8 Sept. 1779.

Bereaved at the loss of her
husband, she died of a
broken heart.

I endeavored to find other plots, those of the Russell men—but my search proved to be fruitless. I was careful to look most closely, but it was vanity. There were no male Russells interred at this place. I vowed that I would find the answer.

I started to return to my horse, when I glanced over and saw the figure of a man standing among the trees. As I started to approach the area, I saw that it was the same apparition that I had encountered earlier at Russell House, the spirit clothed in medieval attire. It stood there, silently, making no movement whatsoever, staring at me. I decided to draw closer, and when I was within ten feet of the figure, it gave this same utterance: "Richard Randolph, touch not the unclean thing and get thee hence from Russell House...," I began to drop to my knees as I stared at the figure, for surely this was no figment of my imagination. After uttering the above warning, the spirit then disappeared. Nevertheless, I was struck with awe, shock, and a feeling of weakness. After about five or six minutes, I rose and returned to my horse, and I then proceeded to return to Russell House. I began to regain my composure along the way, thinking of the incident and also the incident prior to this one.

I could not rationalize it to my satisfaction, but I did realize it was a mystery that I was determined to unravel; and as I thought more of this, it became exciting and it held thoughts of expectation as to what would accompany the exposure of such secrets as this. I began to look upon the coming days at Russell House as being ones of excitement and adventure, such as one would expect, upon the discovery of an old "skeleton in the closet."

I was quite fatigued on my arrival back at Russell House. Nobody was in sight, so I felt like taking a nap, for I was feeling quite fatigued. I went to my room and reclined on the bed. I fell soundly asleep, experiencing a sleep so profoundly deep, and yet, an uncomfortable sleep, one marked by dreams of horrendous nature, nightmares to be exact, so terrible and obtrusive that I recall them to this very day.

At last, I awakened. It was dark, so I must have been asleep for some time. I lit the candle, and it was then that I heard music and the sounds of human voices—sounds of gaiety. I started out of the room, and I noticed that they came forth from the great hall of the house. It was strange music too, not the contemporary music, which I was accustomed to, but music of an earlier age, of the Renaissance or even of an era before that.

I proceeded with great caution and as I neared the hall, I extinguished my candle and put it down, for I wanted to observe the events that were occurring unnoticed. I drew close and peered from behind the drapes mounting both sides of the staircase, for the area was well lighted, with all the candles in the place aflame.

The scene I beheld below is rather hard to describe. There were people in every conceivable costume imaginable, from all periods of time—ranging from recent to several hundred years ago—and yet *all them were women*. All of them save the men in their small, primitive orchestra. Other than that, not a single man among them.

They were all standing around chattering to one another, a group here, a circle there; clearly they were well familiar with each other. I began to doubt my senses, but I couldn't really, for everything was so real. After standing there for several minutes taking care to conceal my presence, I began to feel faint, very weak. I started to steal my way back to my room, only to lie down, for I felt that at any moment I should pass out. I closed the door and fell back into the same deep sleep I had experienced prior to my awakening.

5

Charlotte's Entreaty

The next morning, after rising and getting dressed, I went over every detail of the events that had happened the night before, trying to determine if what happened had actually occurred or if it was all just a bad nightmare. The great hall of the house was still the same as it had been before, i.e., no remnants of merrymaking that are usually left behind the morning after. Indeed, the chandeliers were the same, all covered with dust and cobwebs, thereby giving evidence to their unuse.

However, as I returned to my room, after climbing the stairs, and proceeding down the hallway farther, I turned the corner, and I beheld the spilled candlewax that I distinctly remembered dripping last night after extinguishing my candle and putting it down. I stood there and pondered over this silent evidence, which was difficult to ignore.

I took no breakfast that morning, for I had no hunger nor desire for food. As I stood thinking over what had happened, feelings of hostility and resentment began to swell in my heart, for I began to feel that I had been deceived by the people at Russell House. I felt anger, after my being honest with these people, they should have the audacity to deceive me with a concealment of the truth, after I had sincerely befriended them. Did they regard me as an outsider, one who must be kept in ignorance? To be treated as a dunce? After all, we were cousins, although distant I admit, but, still, as the saying goes, "Blood is thicker than water."

Rage was building up inside me, and I was just waiting for an opportunity to vent my anger on one of them. It was at this time, as I neared the window, that I observed Charlotte in the garden, sitting on the bench near the statue, crying. She was alone, but nevertheless, disturbed about something. I decided to go down immediately.

"What is the matter, Charlotte?" I asked, as I approached. The feelings of hostility built up earlier began to dissipate more into feelings of sympathy, and I thought, *If only she would be honest with me!*

"Really, nothing," was her reply. "I'm just distraught with the condition of Edward." He shows no improvement of course and continues to decline in health."

"Charlotte, I have tried to be friends with you and Edward, and I have been honest about my background and personal history and I believed you had reciprocated, but recent events have led me to believe otherwise. I feel we can be truthful with each other, because, after all, we are cousins."

"What events do you speak of?" she inquired, naïvely.

"Surely, you must know! Strange happenings in this house and on this estate defy the laws of nature. You must admit this; otherwise, the only conclusion is that I suffer from madness. Admit it, this place is haunted."

"Oh, come now," she went on.

"Admit it! Admit it this very instance lest I go this moment and pack my things to leave Russell House! I'll not be treated with deception and fraud by you or anyone!"

"All right," she screamed. "It is true. It has been so for a number of years, and we have suffered the stigma of it to no end. My life has been a Hades ever since childhood." She continued, her voice rising in crescendo. "Do you know what it is like for a child for all her life to suffer the stigma of social ostracism? To never have friends, to never go anywhere without being an object of derision, solely because of the name I possess? Tell me, in all candor, what would you do? How would you feel? Would you never feel the need to withhold the truth at times? Tell me! Tell me!" she screamed accusingly.

She buried her face in her hands, sobbing. "I have never had but one desire in all my life: to leave this place altogether. I have longed to know what the real world is like, what real people do and feel, what it is to be a true person to myself and to others. Take me with you, Richard, from Russell House. Extricate me from this living grave!"

She fell into my arms, crying all the while. "I promise. You will come with me to Boston when I leave."

"What will I do about Edward?" she asked, apprehensively.

"That is a problem we will have to solve in the meantime. Let me think about it before we do anything. Your main priority, I think, is to forget about events in the past, for they are gone forever. Think instead of the happy life that will await you upon leaving here."

It was at this time when I believe I fell fully in love with Charlotte for the first time. Prior to this, I think our relationship was based solely on physical attraction. It is only when one gains an in-depth knowledge into the soul and personality of another that the state of love is achieved.

Because of her honesty with me, it was on this occasion that I knew Charlotte for the first time, i.e., carnal knowledge. For in that kind of relationship one really knows another, physically, intimately, as well as spiritually.

Our love, from that moment onward, became the kind that endures permanently, the kind in which one never wants to be separated from the other. It is the kind of love in which all future events are thought of as happening to each other equally, so that a bond of permanence is achieved, physically as well as emotionally. One feels an emotion of security, a state that is really not evident when one is single. One feels ready to face the world with all its vigors and trials, always confident that both will emerge in a triumph of victory for each other.

This was the life that I envisioned for Charlotte and myself. It was never voiced in words, but one can always sense the emotions and agreement of the other.

6

The Fate of Camelot

Living in a house that is "haunted" can often be a unique experience for the uninitiated. Sometimes, people inhabit or frequent places that are thought haunted, but it is always implied, never admitted. Russell House was different in this respect, as well as others, obviously, The occupants of Russell House had openly admitted this fact, inasmuch as it was evidently well known to the local populace, there was no need to keep it secret, hence the reason for their seclusion and social ostracism.

Most people feel fear and agitation at their sightings of spirits or ghosts or really, any supernatural phenomenon. This, I can say now, was my reaction at first. I soon came to realize that Charlotte had no fear, or no demonstrable fear, although I think it was always latent. Because of this, I felt the need to inquire about what manner one should assume when one is aware of a supernatural presence.

"Exactly what attitude or behavior should I have if I should see a spirit?" I asked Charlotte.

"The best thing to do, I have found, is to simply ignore them. Do not acknowledge their presence. Just ignore them altogether and then, shortly, they usually disappear. One must never display a feeling of fear in their presence.

"Sometimes, it becomes necessary to appease them, if a particularly persistent apparition should appear. These can be both troublesome and difficult to deal with, but rarely have I ever had occasion to encounter such an experience, and I doubt that you will either.

"But, always remember, never purposely provoke or challenge spirits, for it is very dangerous. Many years ago my mother, who was constantly annoyed at this problem, took it upon herself to exorcise one of them. Needless to say, it reacted most violently indeed, destroying all the china and crystal. The entire household was also disrupted at the time with its harassment, e.g., loud noises, screams, and crying. We lost all our servants. They simply were frightened out of their wits, and they ran away and never could be found again. For a long time, we believed we would never be able to possess any more domestic help because of this environment, and it's only because of the exorbitant bribes these demand that we're able to keep them."

During my remaining time at Russell House, some of the happiest days of my life were experienced. We did everything together and we lived every day only for the joy and excitement that being together provided us.

We rode together through the forests, all around the estate, and we went to the old church periodically. It is a very ironic facet of human personality that, although two people are surrounded by a gloomy and melancholy environment, their love permeates each and every circumstance, to the exclusion of sadness altogether. Now, I know how those ancient citizens of Camelot felt, while their kingdom endured. Yet, at the time, I failed to remember that Camelot did not last.

It was agreed upon by both of us, that Edward would be left at Russell House to be cared for by the servant staff, while all financial affairs were to continue to be managed by executors of the estate at the local bank.

Preparations were made for our departure from Russell

House. We were to leave on 2 November, a Monday morning, by carriage to nearby Petersburg, where we would continue by coach onward to Richmond and thence to Boston.

7

The Curse Revealed

During this period leading to our departure from Russell House, our lives were thoroughly involved with each other. Charlotte had ended her reclusion, and all our time was preoccupied with each other.

The Sunday morning prior to our departure was different. I couldn't find Charlotte. I searched throughout the house and the grounds, but she was not to be found. As I passed the northeastern perimeter of the house, I noticed at the same uppermost window, the outline of a man, staring out the window into space. Could it be Edward? It did not seem to resemble him, although I really couldn't tell because of the great distance at which I stood. Nevertheless, I didn't have time to draw closer to ascertain who it was, because the curtain was soon drawn. Of the rooms at Russell House, I had been in all of them save this one, and it was now my intention to determine its contents.

I entered the house and unexpectedly met Charlotte. "Where have you been?" I demanded. "I've looked everywhere."

"I've been in my room," she said sheepishly.

"No, you haven't. I looked there."

"Richard, I want to tell you something that has been troubling me for a long time."

"Let me hear it."

"Do you think it's possible for me not to really be in love with you after all? If I left with you, and I saw what the world was actually like, with other people and other men, do you think it possible that I should cease to love you, that this has been only infatuation, not really love? You must realize that you are the only man who has ever had the opportunity to show any interest in me. You are the only person of the opposite sex whom I've actually ever known, except servants. And when a man shows such intense interest in such a naïve and sheltered woman, surely she is flattered and infatuated, but is it truly love?"

"I really don't know," I responded. "I guess only time will tell."

"Yes, time will tell, but that is what I'm afraid of. Prior to your coming here, I was virtually a prisoner, and I don't want you to ever think that I intentionally used you."

"I'll never think that, I promise."

"I want to tell you now, truthfully from my heart, I would never do anything, purposely, that would hurt you or cause you ignominy. Do you believe me?"

"Of course, I do," I replied, taking her in my arms.

"If anything should ever happen to me or if I should ever do anything that is wrong, would you disown me? Would you abhor me?"

"Of course not. Don't think about such things that will never happen. You have only happiness to look forward to, nothing else."

"Richard, this is my last day at Russell House, and if you don't mind, I'd like to be by myself. I want to reflect on the life that I'll be leaving and the new life I will be going to." With a kiss I left her.

I spent the rest of the day in my room. As dusk approached, I thought I should find Charlotte. When I went to look for her, I noticed she was in the garden, on the same bench, near the statue, weeping into her handkerchief, with great grief. Indeed, one would think she was losing a loved one instead of proceeding to a new life. I made no attempt to go to her. My feelings were entirely passive. At this moment, I felt like a stranger, intruding into the private domain of a family into which I had no right to enter.

I stood there, watching this scene, for nearly twenty minutes, when at last, she started to the livery stable. It was now dark, but I had made up my mind to follow her. I knew where she intended to go, and I was determined to follow her, to find out what this great secrecy was about. After she departed, I hastened to saddle my horse and I rode to the old church! Now, at last, I presumed, I would finally be privy to the secret of Russell House! I was filled with excitement and expectation at what I would find.

I tied my horse far away from the church, and I then advanced towards it. It was a clear night, and all the tombstones glistened in the moonlight. I passed her horse, which was tied much closer, and slowly walked to the old structure, taking care not to stumble or to make any noise that would reveal my presence. I could see there was a light inside, although faint, and I crept up to one of the windows, which were now just open spaces.

There was Charlotte, with two or three candles lit, writing upon the white plastered wall with a pencil. She evidently already knew what she was writing, for she continued in bold style, never hesitating one second as to what she was inscribing. I gazed on this scene with complete awe and bewilderment, at times even holding my breath, lest my very breathing should reveal my presence!

At last, she finally departed. I concealed my presence during her leaving, for I wanted to behold this sight myself. At length, when I was sure she was in fact gone, I crept in, lighted the remaining candles, and stared at the inscription:

27

Thou art crumbling to the dust,
old pile,
Thou art hastening to thy fall,
And 'round thee in thy loneliness
Clings the ivy to thy wall.
The worshipers are scattered now,
Who knelt before thy shrine,
And silence reigns where anthems
rose
In days of "Auld Lang Syne."

And sadly sighs the wandering
wind
Where oft in years gone by
Prayers rose from many hearts
to Him
The Highest of the High;
The tramp of many a busy foot
That sought they aisles is o'er
And many a weary heart around
Is still forevermore.

How doth ambition's hope take
wing.
How droops the spirit now;
We hear the distant city's din.
The dead are mute below.
The sun that shone upon their
paths
Now gilds their lonely graves;
The zephyrs which once fanned
their brows
The grass above them waves.

Oh! Could we call the many back
Who've gathered here in vain—
Who've careless roved where we
do now,
Who'll never meet again;
How would our very hearts be
stirred
To meet the earnest gaze
Of the lovely and the beautiful
The lights of other days.

My heart was touched by pity and sympathy for Charlotte. With what remorse and grief she must be afflicted! And with such heroic elegance, even to rival Homer, did she express it. I stood there reflecting on this scene, trying to affix an interpretation or meaning to it.

At length, I rode back to Russell House in somber spirits, not knowing what to expect. The weather had now changed, for the winds were blowing, altering the forms of the forest into grotesque shapes and figures. I had the foreboding of something evil, but what it was I knew not. It seemed to me that the spirits of Russell House were antagonized by my presence, and I felt guilty that I had trespassed onto something forbidden, but what it was, of course, I had no knowledge of. I felt myself being drawn unto Russell House, being summoned as if for judgment.

I rode directly to the front, tied my horse and entered. The sight I beheld is still fixed in my mind to this very day. There was the same spirit that I had encountered in my first days at Russell House, hovering in the air, at least six feet in stature. with Charlotte standing in front below, at the foot of the stairs.

I said nothing. Charlotte addressed me. "Richard, I have not been truthful with you; rather, I have deceived you all along. I cannot go with you from Russell House. Though with all my heart I love you, still, I cannot allow myself to inflict this evil upon you by marriage."

"Of what evil do you speak?" I timidly responded.

At this, Charlotte dropped to her knees, crying. Then the apparition began to speak, in the same somber tones in which it had addressed me earlier:

"Richard Randolph, you heeded not your warning to leave Russell House. Therefore, you marry into this family at your own peril. This line is forever cursed, from times ancient, until the extinction of the line of their family, because of the ignominy and treason of their forefather, Harold Godwineson.

"When our beloved and saintly King, Edward the Confessor, who once ruled our English nation with Christian devotion and sanctity, departed this life, it was his desire that the throne should pass to his rightful heir and cousin, William, Duke of Normandy.

"By right, the throne belonged to William, and Harold affirmed this, under holy oath and honorable promise to William. Yet, when King Edward died, Harold broke his sacred promise, and assumed the throne, thus provoking invasion of England and needless devastation of our land and people.

"At Hastings, Harold was killed, and his male descendants are doomed forever to wretched disease, and those who marry into this family are doomed to wander in perpetuity, to compensate for the malefaction of their forefather, Harold."

With this revelation, the ghost disappeared, and I was once again left alone with Charlotte.

"Is it true?" I implored with faint heart.

"It is, and I have not had the courage to tell you. But

30

now, you must see, your eyes must behold the curse that afflicts us to this very day. Come with me."

She led me to that uppermost room, to which I never had gained entrance. She unlocked it, and with great apprehension, she lighted the candles.

The sight that I beheld was frightening and horrendous. All around the room were bodies, preserved in some manner, their features all in ghoulish and abominable forms. I raised my hand, seemingly to shield my face from the despicable, evil forms, as if they were Satan himself. They were all dressed in clothes of different periods, some hanging on the wall, others lying next to each other. The memory of the loathsome creatures haunts my mind to this very day.

"This is the curse that we carry," Charlotte cried, "that our male offspring should be afflicted with disease that ossifies body parts while in the peak of their manhood. The onset is insidious. It begins with a slight lameness, such as Edward now has. Gradually, over a period of usually three years, with great pain and suffering, parts of their bodies become ossified, until it strikes a vital organ, when they expire. They never decay in the ordinary manner; rather, they remain preserved in this manner, their horrible and corrupt features evident to anyone who might behold them. It is forbidden for them to be buried in holy ground."

With tears in her eyes, she continued. "This is why I cannot marry, for to marry you would inflict evil upon you and upon our children, and you, too, would become an untouchable, even as I am, shunned by people, rather, hated by them for something over which I had no control. In years past, these marriages were to cousins who lived here and in this vicinity, and they were accustomed to this, but they are gone now, and you are an innocent, one who has not been touched by this infamy.

"Edward and I are the last Russells. We shall not marry, because we have decided that this curse will die with us, for we are the last of the line of Harold Godwineson, and we intend that this evil shall end forever without our posterity, and then the stigma will be gone and forgotten, like all of those who have gone before us. Leave Russell House, Richard, forever leave me and these memories behind and you will not be hurt; you will not be touched by this evil. But be assured, dear Richard, that I shall always remember you and your love and kindness with which I have been blessed. Leave, Richard! Leave Russell House!" she hysterically demanded.

I did. I left Russell House without further ado, and I rode off into the darkness, overcome by what I had just witnessed, numb in spirit and heart, half-believing what had just happened there in the last few hours.

Epilogue

Many years have elapsed since my abrupt departure from Russell House. I never heard again from Charlotte, nor did I attempt to communicate with her. I do not know what has become of Russell House or its inhabitants, nor have I read anything pertaining to the subject.

Everyone knows the tragic story of King Harold II (Harold Godwineson) and the events leading to his death in 1066 at Hastings. Indeed, his actions brought about the only successful invasion of England in almost a millennium. Did his family continue to suffer after Hastings? The sons of Harold are last mentioned in recorded history in June 1069, when they led an invasion force off the coast of North Devon. The invasion was soundly defeated, but the historical record informs us that they escaped, unharmed.

Did the inhabitants of Russell House die unmarried, as they wished? Or did they go elsewhere and continue to exist, in the safety of a new identity and location? If so, did they ever find true peace and privacy? I cannot say.

Nevertheless, I shall never return to Virginia, but sometimes, or should I say often, to be truthful, my thoughts return there, especially in autumn. My thoughts return to the old church, to Russell House and to Charlotte. I can still see her riding through the forest, and I think of the happiness we shared together for that short period.

No, I was not touched by the curse at Russell House; nonetheless, I too shall remember you, Charlotte, and your love until the end of my days.